JE   19

THE SMUSHY BUS

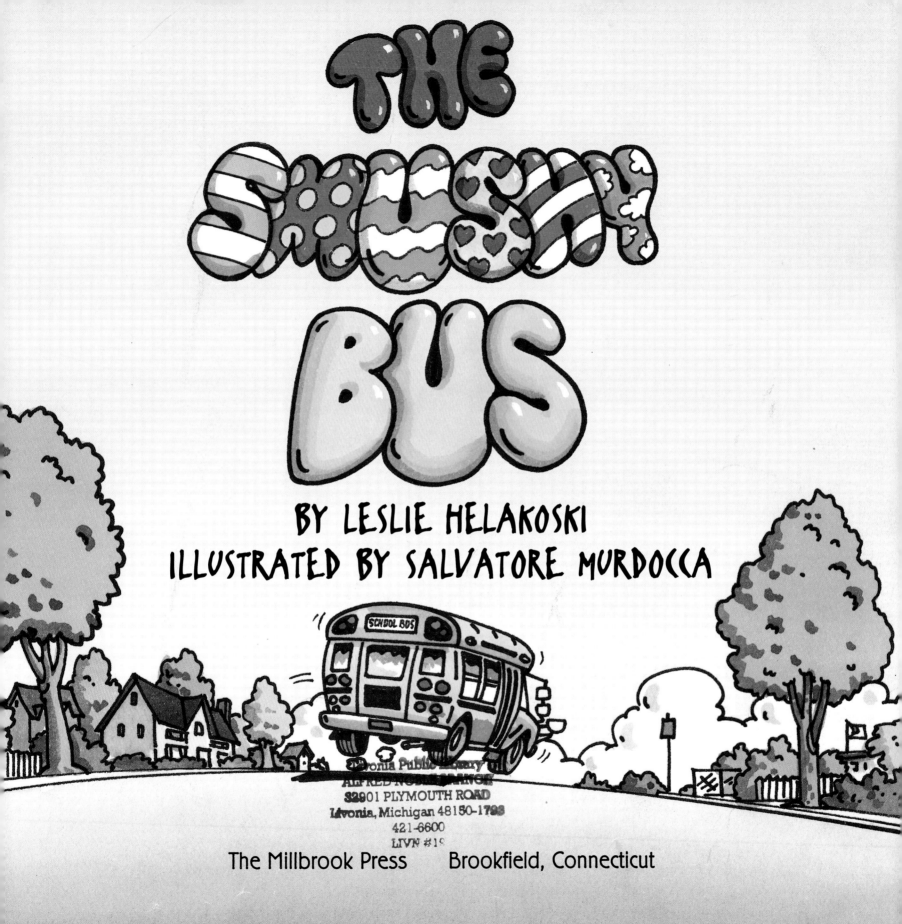

BY LESLIE HELAKOSKI

ILLUSTRATED BY SALVATORE MURDOCCA

The Millbrook Press   Brookfield, Connecticut

To the old man on the mountain—LH

For Sergei—SM

The school bus was late.

The children from Addington Elementary School were waiting to go home. The kindergartners were starting to cry. The grade oners were hanging in and out of the mimosa trees. The grade twoers were shooting spitballs at the grade oners. The grade threers were playing hide-and-seek in the bushes. The grade fours were jumping out of the school windows. The grade fivers were playing dodgeball. The teachers were frantic.

Finally, up chugged a tiny little school bus.

"Sorry I'm late," Mr. Mathers called out. "Our regular bus is at the repair shop."

Mr. Mathers looked at all the children. He looked at the little bus with only four seats. "Now, this is a problem," he said. "But I will get them all home in time for supper."

"We're counting on it," said the teachers as they leaped for their cars.

16 kindergartners were trying to get on the bus. Looking around, Mr. Mathers noticed 8 bookshelves above the seats. He slid 2 kindergartners, toes in first, onto each shelf. They were a bit slippery from crying so they fit in quite easily.

The 12 grade oners were scrambling out of the trees and racing to the bus. Mr. Mathers had them all stop and untie their shoes. Using the laces, he tied the children into stacks of 3. He made 4 stacks and put one stack under each seat of the bus.

Mr. Mathers turned to the grade twoers. There were 13 of them. "Hmm. That's odd," mumbled Mr. Mathers. He crunched 3 children onto each seat with their knees up. 3 grade twoers on 4 seats made 12 grade twoers. Mr. Mathers had 1 child left over. "You are what we call a remainder," he said to the child. "Just hang around over here, and we'll deal with you later."

"Now, what shall I do with 16 grade threers?" asked Mr. Mathers. He measured the space behind each of the 4 seats. There was enough room for 4 grade threers to slide in sideways if one stuck his head and one arm out the window. "Hang on tight," he said.

Next, Mr. Mathers marched all 11 grade fours down the aisle. When they turned around, he gave the one in front a push and they fell, like dominoes, on one another's laps—all, that is, except Buster, who was wider than the aisle. Mr. Mathers had to substitute 2 grade twoers for Buster and put Buster in a seat.

Mr. Mathers added the 8 grade fivers to the top of the bus. "Lock elbows with the person next to you," he called.

Numbers were bouncing around Mr. Mathers' head. When he counted all the kids he had smushed on the bus, his total was 76. "Well, that sums that up," he said to himself as he drove off.

The bus was full. It teetered around corners. It climbed steep hills. It bounced over bumps in the road. The children hung on.

When the bus stopped at First Street, 76 children groaned.

Mr. Mathers opened the doors, and 15 children tumbled out. "Now, how many kids are left on the bus?" he asked.

"What's the difference?" wailed a crushed grade threer.

"Exactly," said Mr. Mathers. He wrote the numbers in the dust of his window.

When the bus stopped at Second Street, 61 children groaned.
16 children jumped out of the windows, and 5 children slid off the top
of the bus. "Be sure to use the proper steps," said Mr. Mathers.

When the bus stopped at Third Street, 40 children groaned. Mr. Mathers let out $1/2$ of the kids. He handed one kid his backpack and his baseball. "Try to remember everything you carried," Mr. Mathers said.

When the bus stopped at Fourth Street, 20 children groaned.
12 children jammed the aisle trying to get out. "Always keep things
lined up," pointed out Mr. Mathers. The children straightened up
their line and moved correctly off the bus.

When the bus stopped at Fifth Street, 8 children cheered. 7 children got off the bus. "It was nothing," said Mr. Mathers. "Always go back and check for anything you may have forgotten," he told them when he found a lunchbox under one of the seats.

Mr. Mathers drove away. "That was quite a test, but I got all those children home in time for supper," he said proudly. "I shouldn't have any more problems to solve for the remainder of the day."

ABOUT THE AUTHOR AND ILLUSTRATOR

This is a first book for Leslie Helakoski, who worked in advertising and design before becoming a writer. She grew up in Louisiana, where she always rode a bus to school and always searched for ways to make math fun. Currently she is painting as well as writing. She lives in Michigan with her husband and three children.

Salvatore Murdocca has been illustrating and writing books for children for many years. His latest Millbrook picture books are BIG NUMBERS and LITTLE NUMBERS both by Edward Packard, and DOUBLE TROUBLE IN WALLA WALLA by Andrew Clements. He is the illustrator of the Magic Treehouse series of books and the author-illustrator of LUCY TAKES A HOLIDAY and TUTTLE'S SHELL.

Sal and his wife Nancy, a textile designer, live in Rockland County, New York. They are avid runners and have toured Europe on bicycles.

Library of Congress Cataloging-in-Publication Data
Helakoski, Leslie.
The smushy bus / by Leslie Helakoski ; illustrated by Salvatore Murdocca.
p. cm.
Summary: When the regular schoolbus is in the shop, a clever driver must use all that he knows about addition and subtraction to ensure that seventy-six children get on—and off—of the four-seat substitute bus.
ISBN 0-7613-1398-2 (lib. bdg.) – ISBN 0-7613-1917-4 (trade)
[1. School buses—Fiction. 2. Bus drivers—Fiction. 3. Addition.
4. Subtraction.] I. Murdocca, Salvatore, ill. II. Title.
PZ7.H37275 Sm 2002   [E]–dc21   2002001929

Published by The Millbrook Press, Inc.
2 Old New Milford Road, Brookfield, Connecticut 06804
www.millbrookpress.com

Printed in Hong Kong
5 4 3 2 1 (lib. bdg.)
5 4 3 2 1 (trade)